The Flying Spring Onion

Matthew Sweeney was born in Donegal in 1952 and has lived in London since 1973. He works increasingly in schools, both primary and secondary, encouraging children to write, and has two children of his own. He also writes for adults.

The Flying Spring Onion

MATTHEW SWEENEY

Illustrated by David Austen

faber and faber

LONDON · BOSTON

First published in 1992
by Faber and Faber Ltd
3 Queen Square London WC1N 3AU

Phototypeset by Wilmaset, Birkenhead, Wirral
Printed in Great Britain by
Cox & Wyman Ltd, Reading, Berkshire

A CIP record for this book is available from the British Library

ISBN 0-571-16172-3

For Nico and Malvin,
who read or heard these first

Contents

The Flying Spring Onion

The flying spring onion
   flew through the air
      over to where
the tomatoes grew in rows
   and he said to those
      seed-filled creatures
My rooted days are done,
   so while you sit here
      sucking sun
I'll be away and gone,
   to Greenland
   where they eat no green
      and I won't be seen
in a salad bowl with you,
   stung by lemon,
      greased by oil,
and nothing at all to do
   except wait to be eaten.
With that he twirled
   his green propellers
and rose above the rows
   of red balls
who stared as he grew small
   and disappeared.

Cows on the Beach

Two cows,
fed-up with grass, field, farmer,
barged through barbed wire
and found the beach.
Each mooed to each:
This is a better place to be,
a stretch of sand next to the sea,
this is the place for me.
And they stayed there all day,
strayed this way, that way,
over to rocks,
past discarded socks,
ignoring the few people they met
(it wasn't high season yet).
They dipped hooves in the sea,
got wet up to the knee,
they swallowed pebbles and sand,
found them a bit bland,
washed them down with sea-water,
decided they really ought to
rest for an hour.
Both were sure
they'd never leave here.
Imagine, they'd lived so near
and never knew!
With a swapped moo
they sank into sleep,
woke to the yellow jeep
of the farmer

revving there
feet from the incoming sea.
This is no place for cows to be,
he shouted, and slapped them
with seaweed, all the way home.

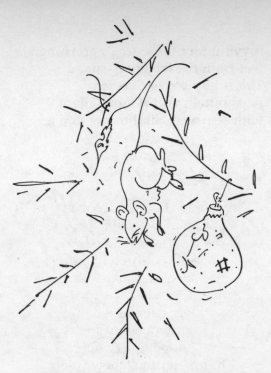

The Mouse and the Xmas Tree

The mouse ran up the Xmas tree
        hey ho, hey ho,
through a well-lit, uphill forest
        that wasn't there before,
and he thought: all these bells
and stars, and deer and dwarves
        are brill and honey-dandy
and I'll nibble some to prove it,
but as I alone can climb the tree
        I am still the best.

And through the tree's green needles
    came the mouse's song:
        Hey ho, hey ho,
I'm fed up with the floor.
I'm even more bored
    with the world behind
        the skirting-board.
I like this stood-up wood.

And he ran on up that Xmas tree
    as fast as he could
and the bells blocked his way,
    the lights burned his sides,
    the needles pricked his fur,
but still he reached the top
where the angel was waiting
    to kick him, squealing,
        hey ho, hey ho,
    bumpety, scratchety, plop,
onto the needle-strewn floor
    where he'd been before
        and where he'd stay.

Fishbones Dreaming

Fishbones lay in the smelly bin.
He was a head, a backbone and a tail.
Soon the cats would be in for him.

He didn't like to be this way.
He shut his eyes and dreamed back.

Back to when he was fat, and hot on a plate.
Beside green beans, with lemon juice
squeezed on him. And a man with a knife
and fork raised, about to eat him.

He didn't like to be this way.
He shut his eyes and dreamed back.

Back to when he was frozen in the freezer.
With lamb cutlets and minced beef and prawns.
Three months he was in there.

He didn't like to be this way.
He shut his eyes and dreamed back.

Back to when he was squirming in a net,
with thousands of other fish, on the deck
of a boat. And the rain falling
wasn't wet enough to breathe in.

He didn't like to be this way.
He shut his eyes and dreamed back.

Back to when he was darting through the sea,
past crabs and jellyfish, and others
like himself. Or surfacing to jump for flies
and feel the sun on his face.

He liked to be this way.
He dreamed hard to try and stay there.

Catching Squid

I caught a squid on a line –
I was sitting on a rock,
a white rock, long and shiny.
The water was green and frothy
and smelt of apples,
and the squid was on my line.
I happen to like squid –
didn't think I would
till my Dad cooked them.
He told me then you don't
catch squid on lines,
but *I* did. Doesn't matter
that my squid is rubber
and was a present. Doesn't
matter that the line
is a length of twine
that I tied on the squid,
then dropped it in the bath.
I still caught a squid on a line
and the squid was mine.

My Dog John

My dog John is a poodle
who sits in the bath all day,
        staring
        at the air-vent
on the bathroom's red wall,
as if he'd been sent
a picture, by telepathy,
        of a butterfly
        winging
its fluttery paper way
from the hole in the wall
to the mouth of a poodle,
        a poodle named John.

But hang on, son.
John's no name for a poodle.
And he wouldn't eat butterflies,
and if he sat in the bath all day
he'd drown!
Ah, but, Mister,
the bath's kept dry,
and even I eat butterflies,
and my name is John,
a good sound,
don't you think, Sir,
an excellent name, I'd say,
ESPECIALLY FOR A POODLE!

James's Mum

On the day he was ten years old
James was told
he couldn't keep monkeys any more.
What's a spare bedroom for?
Besides, he only had three.
Was he to set them free?
Who cared if they messed their room?
It wasn't a tomb.
They were living.
James was forgiving
as long as they played with him.
But Mum wanted rid of them,
wanted them on the street,
wanted clean carpet under her feet
in the sitting room,
in the spare bedroom –
anywhere in the house.
She said he could buy a mouse
as long as he bought a cage.
James flew into a rage,
jumped up on the table,
whistled as loud as he was able
till the monkeys hurtled in.
James raised his chin
and pointed at Mum.
Each of the three bit her bum.
Mum ran, screaming, from the house.
'That's what you get for your talk of a mouse!'
James shouted after her,

and there was monkey laughter for
at least an hour.
Then James grew dour
at the thought of Mum's return.
He thought he might burn
the house down.
He realised with a frown
the monkeys had to be gone
when she got home.
Do you want some?
Three, or two, or one?
Hurry up and tell him.
Quickly, here comes Mum.

Into the Mixer

Into the mixer he went,
    the nosy boy,
into the mess of wet cement,
    round and round
    with a glugging sound
and a boyish screamed complaint.

Out of the mixer he came,
    the concrete boy,
onto the road made of the same
    quick-setting stuff.
    He looked rough
and he'd only himself to blame.

Johnjoe's Snowman

Johnjoe built a snowman
shaped like a wigwam
and postbox-sized.

What he didn't tell
was that inside the snowman
he'd stuffed the cat.

All Sunday morning
he patted with his shovel
the sides of that snowman.

He didn't bother with a head.
He'd never seen a snowman
that looked real yet.

How was it a snowman?
Because Johnjoe said so,
and he should know.

When it was finished
he stared at the snowman
and saw it wasn't right.

What the world didn't need
(apart from frozen cats)
was another white snowman.

In memory of the cat
he took the snowman
and sprayed it black.

Blue Hair

In between the dinner ladies
runs the blue-haired boy,
spilling beans and jelly,
and all us kids are yelling
'Catch him! Catch Blue Hair!'
though mostly we like him,
would like to be like him
but wouldn't dare. And look,
he's out front again –
the forks are clattering down –
and haring past our tables,
our laughing, screaming tables,
with five teachers in pursuit
(they'll never catch Blue Hair!).
And none of us can eat,
we're banging with our spoons,
blowing with our breaths,
erupting in a roar
as Blue Hair dodges everyone
and bursts out the door.

The Card

Who sent the card where a blue baboon
   sits on a red bike, and wrote inside
      'Happy Birthday, Sid'?

They know I'm not Sid, 'coz my real name
   (which I'm not telling you) was outside
      on the green envelope,

but no address or stamp was there, so
   they shoved it in the letterbox
      and scarpered.

So they know me, and they know my birthday
   ain't now, and if *they* know me
      I know *them*

even if I can't put a face to them just yet
   but they forget that I'm a detective
      with a bad temper.

They're just jealous of my red bike that beats
   their rattleboxes in every race
      while I never sweat.

They don't know that I love baboons, and go
   to speak to them in their language
      at the zoo –

that I think more highly of blue baboons
  than I do of them, with their wedge
    haircuts, and Reeboks.

But I'm not going to tell them this, no way —
  or maybe I will, after I've
    made them sorry.

My Dear Mungo

My dear Mungo,
it's time you went away –
cleared off to Canada,
there to stay,
up in the tundra
of the frozen North –
Queen Elizabeth Islands
or worse,
where no-one lives
except snowy bears
and long-toothed walruses
and snowier hares –
only up there
could I like you,
send me a snapshot
so I can see you
just as you'll be,
hair past your chin,
a glint in your eye
and ice on your grin,
mouthing your insults
and smart remarks
to leopard seals
and prowling sharks –
my dear Mungo,
head for Heathrow,
I've had it, mate,
beat it, go!

Night Boy

After the cat went out
and the moon sat on the hill
and the sea drowned a lorry
that broke down
                    stealing sand,
little, skinny George awoke.

He was little, because he hardly grew.
He hardly grew, because he ate
scraps of chicken, leftover rice, dry bread,
what was left on the dog's plate,
handfuls of cornflakes, jam.
That may sound a lot
but it left George little and skinny.

What about mealtimes? I hear you ask.
Mealtimes, for George, were sleeptimes
most of the year. That's right,
he slept all day,
                    got up at night.

What about school? you're saying.
I know, I know what you're like.
What do you know about stars?
Does the sea glow at night
like a green watch-dial?
Ask George, he'll tell you.
He'll even write it down
and read it to you, by torchlight,
and then he'll count the stars.

Blame the holidays, his Gran said,
they're too long.
George lived with his Gran,
George, the sleeper-in
who'd slept in so long, so often,
that now he woke at night
when Gran was asleep.

What did he do at night?
He went to the beach,
lit driftwood fires,
stood in a cave and waited
for spies in submarines
to land.
        He climbed hills
and aeroplane-spotted,
especially small ones
landing in fields.

He hid in ditches
and eavesdropped on strangers.
He woke the neighbour's donkey
and galloped round the field.

He lay on a haystack
and watched the dawn.
Then he yawned
              and went to bed.

And if he met Gran on the stairs,
Good day, was what he said.

A Town Called Heaven

'One mile to Heaven'
said the signpost
and a voice from a speaker
said the same.
And in the distance
half hidden by trees
he saw roofs and lampposts
and began to run.

'One mile to Heaven'
said the voice again.
One mile, he thought,
and slowed down.
He was in no hurry.

He liked trees.
He thought about 'Heaven'
as the name for a town.

Who'd called it that?
Who could live there?
What if they were bad?
Did people die there?
'One mile to Heaven'
said the voice again
but quieter, now
that the roofs had grown.

He shook his smiling head
on the street of Heaven.
He'd imagined free sweets
and model trains.
He found a town
much like his own
and posted a letter
to his Mum.

Note: In the Black Forest, in Germany, there is a town called
Heaven.

All the Dogs

You should have seen him –
he stood in the park and whistled,
underneath an oak tree,
and all the dogs came bounding up
and sat around him,
keeping their big eyes on him,
tails going like pendulums.

And there was one cocker pup
who went and licked his hand,
and a labrador who whimpered
till the rest joined in.
Then he whistled a second time,
high-pitched as a stoat,
over all the shouted dog names
and whistles of owners,
till a flurry of paws
brought more dogs, panting,
as if they'd come miles,
and these too found space
on the flattened grass
to stare at the boy's
unmemorable face
which all the dogs found special.

Jan

Meet Jan, he lives on the top of a hill
with a pet goat he won't name
and a white hen he treats the same.
If you won't meet him, others will –

like Norman Bates over there, talking
to the girl with orange hair,
he's already been up there
at Jan's. Ask him, he'll tell you walking

is the only way to get there,
the road stops a mile back,
and then you stand and hack
through rhododendrons, and there

in front of you, is Jan's windmill
painted black, with sails turning
to keep Jan's lights burning
and his hi-fi playing. Come on, he'll

greet you with goat's milk, and eggs
and maybe fresh fruit
from his plot, but no meat.
Keep your eye off his hen's legs.

Look, instead, at how fit Jan is
up there on his hill farm
doing the world no harm –
the world that could live as Jan does.

The Field

Where the boy sees cattle
there was a battle
but the boy doesn't know it.
How could he know it?
He sees a field,
no sign of a shield
or an axe, or a sword,
not a cross word,
not a single shout,
just grass on the snout
of a bullock
as he stands on a rock,
chewing,
then mooing
till the boy walks on.
But when the sun
sinks in the sea
the boy would see,
instead of a farmer,
ghosts in armour
on ghost-horses.
He'd hear curses,
and the night-sky
miles high
would ring with steel
striking steel,
and the ghostly dead
and the odd head

would lie on the ground,
but not a sound
will the boy hear.
He won't be near.
He'll be home in bed,
as good as dead.

Sing

'Sing something!' roared the monk,
as he pulled the horse's reins
and brought the creature to a stop
outside the village sweet-shop
where children loitered in the rain.

'Sing something! Sing it now!
I've galloped here from France
through four nights and five days.
I started in a heat-haze.
Sing, and do a sun-dance!'

He sat there on his worn horse
and all the children stared,
then one young skinhead sang
a frantic scrap of rock-song
so loud the horse reared

and dumped the monk in mud.
But a smile broke on his beard.
He had his song, and the prance
of the horse was his sun-dance.
And sure enough, the sky cleared.

The Music

In the distance music was escaping –
from an open window?
The girl heard it, and was outside,
and even though it was raining,
she was away through the trees.

Come back, her mother called after her
but it was no use –
it was the girl's music, what she liked,
and soon she was gone from sight
and night was coming down.

Have you ever been in a forest at dusk,
those faces in the trees . . . ?
The girl didn't notice, didn't need light
to lead her flying feet
over the twigs without a sound.

And when she came to the rope-ladder
dangling from the dark,
its end was luminous, and she went up
to where the music was loud
and every note rippled through her.

And as she passed over her mother
still calling her name,
she heard nothing, and saw nothing
as she zoomed through the sky
in the music that was hers.

Lucy's Gosling

Lucy calls her gosling Mona
and takes her for walks by the sea.
There is such a wet lot of sea
all around Lucy, all around.

You got it, she lives on an island,
an island named Glashedy.

Out there the ships criss-cross
and never come near.
Lucy wouldn't want them near,
nor would Mona.

It's crowded enough on the island,
the island named Glashedy.

There's Dad, when he's not fishing.
There's Mona and Lucy.
There's Mona and Lucy.
Oh, and there's Grandpa in the cave.

Yes, there's a cave on the island,
the island named Glashedy.

I bet you like going in caves.
This one's where Lucy sleeps,
where Mona, Dad and Grandpa sleep
in the quiet and the sea air.

Imagine, no traffic on the island,
the island named Glashedy.

Lucy's Grandpa eyes her gosling.
Says he's fed up with fish,
nothing to eat but fish.
Lucy tells him 'Eat yourself.'

A gosling is quite safe on the island,
the island named Glashedy.

OK, a girl with a gosling,
but won't the gosling grow?
So what? Lucy will grow
into a big girl with a goose.

And they'll grow old on the island,
the island named Glashedy.

Me and Benjy

Me and Benjy, my teddybear,
went to bed to sleep.
What else would we do but sleep?
We couldn't, however –
the noise was atrocious,
shouting and laughing,
thumping and whooping –
Just imagine if that was us,
I whispered in Benjy's ear,
Guzzling wine and beer,
making one hell of a fuss!
What are we going to do?
I looked into Benjy's eyes,
Benjy's brownglass eyes.
Benjy, it has to be you,
I said, throwing him out,
then sliding out myself,
knocking a book from a shelf
with a thump, and a shout
from downstairs: *Go to sleep!*

The cheek of it, I thought.
One of their party ought
to investigate sleep-
possibilities up here,
to lie down on our bed,
pull the pillow over her head,
and ignore down there!
Come on Benjy, let's go.
We crept down the stairs,
me and that Benjybear,
and walked on tiptoe
to the living-room din
that vibrated the floor.
I pulled open the door
and chucked Benjy in.

Eclipse

We watched the moon's eclipse
and no-one knew.

We set the clock and buried it
in Nathan's pillow.

We dressed, and climbed out
onto the flat roof.

Look, said Sid. *There's a bite
out of the moon.*

A bite! said Nathan. *Some dog!*
But Sid's bite grew

and seemed to me more like
night's takeover,

perhaps for ever – moon dissolved
by space-acid,

earth next . . . I shook my head.
Nightdreaming!

Sid was snoring. Nathan woke him,
glanced behind.

I stared at the bright sliver
the moon was.

Then it was gone. All dark –
then it was back,

or another sliver, the other side
of the moon.

And when it looked on course
for roundness

we climbed inside, and were asleep
in minutes.

Were still asleep at breakfast.
Didn't tell why.

Ghost-Train

There's blood on the ghost-train
as it rattles past the mad barber,
but it's real blood – those sharp tops
of coke cans – and Dracula
doesn't have band-aid or antiseptic,
and the pirate in the wrecked ship
is waving his cutlass and shouting
he wants to get you, to cut you more,
while up on the ceiling are bats –
you know there are, and nothing
wakes them quicker than blood,
its cloying aroma spreading through air
just like its red fills water –
and right then a head falls,
bouncing off the train, and the howl
of a ghost echoes ahead
into the sunlight that blinds you
as the train judders to a stop
and you look at your thumb
and only now shove it in your mouth.

Man on the Line

When the toothbrush hit the teeth
            the phone rang.
It was early, but not too early.
Oh, let's be honest, it was late!

'Are you quite awake?' a voice said,
            a man's voice.
'I, myself, have finished lunch,
I was chewing while you were snoring.'

She held the receiver away from her,
            she stared at it
and went to put it gently down.
'Don't hang up on me,' he shouted,

this man on the end of the line.
            Who was he?
'It doesn't matter who I am,
I've a bone to pick with you.

'What do you think you're doing
            sleeping late?
Think of what you missed this morning,
think of all you could have done.

'I, myself, don't sleep now.
            I gave it up.
Know what I call a night's sleep?
Another little slice of death.

'I know *you* need some sleep.
                    Most do.
But don't overdo it, don't be greedy,
jump up early, get out there.'

The man on the line hung up.
                    She did too
and tiptoed down the stairs to bed
to rest, to clear her ringing head.

On the Stairs

She sat all alone on the stairs
outside her door. No-one was in,
except for Fred downstairs
who'd let her in. Come on, Mum,
get back home, climb those stairs
that, you say, keep you thin!
Where was Mum? She should be in.

She fidgeted on the stairs
outside her door. The parrot was in
but couldn't flap downstairs
to let her in, couldn't phone
for help, or keys, or Mum.
The stares she'd endured
walking home alone!

Why hadn't Mum phoned
if she wasn't going to be in?
Mum, who was used to stares
and who usually walked her home.
Who walked to keep thin.
She sat at the top of the stairs
and waited. Mum, walk in!

The Doctor's Son

'Look how the doctor's son
sits at the front of the church,
wears a tie every day.
Watch how he smiles
and greets the passers-by
in the mildest way.
Couldn't you think of *him*
instead of the rest of them
when you want to play?
Couldn't you learn
to be a bit like him,
and mind what you say?
I've heard he really swots
while you and your tramp-friends
waste the day.

'He'll be a doctor too,
a surgeon perhaps,
while you and them stay
forever round here,
jobless, no doubt,
grown men at play.
Catch hold of yourself,
look at the doctor's boy
and lean that way.'

'I see the doctor's son
and I'd very much like
to chuck him into the sea.'

The City of Waste

In the city of waste
lights on the street stay on all day
and children do nothing but play.
What's wrong with that?
                    I hear you say.

Listen, listen to that guitarist
on the cassette.
How do you think you get
to be that good?
You gotta work, that's right, work.
Then you enjoy your play.

Look, look at that goalie
on the telly.
Do you think you make those saves
without practice?
You gotta work, that's right, work.
Then you enjoy your play.

Music? Football?
They're not work, you say.
They're part of your play.
You wear a Walkman and hum.
You bang a ball against a wall.

Aha, I know you do
and they did too
but look at them and look at you.

And the lights on the street are for night.
It's the sun's turn in the day.

No Rider

Boys on bicycles were on the street,
out for the morning, not expecting to meet
a horse with no rider trotting along
with its head high, as if nothing was wrong,
as if no trousered bum on its back
were normal, as if the absolute lack
of a heavy, human, reins-pulling weight
was the correct horsey state.

And the more the boys stared the more they agreed
that this was a surefooted steed
that knew exactly where it was going,
and at once they began following,
down through the village, past the clock,
past shoppers frozen in shock
as horse and bikes entered the churchyard
and stopped at a grave where the horse neighed hard.

Worrying Days

By now the donkey knew
he was safe from the stew.
He was old,
he was easily cold.
He had a wonky heart,
he could hardly pull the olive cart,
but at least he wouldn't fill
the casserole
all winter.
Worrying days were over.

And on the shore road
with a light load
of driftwood
he felt he could
gallop across Sicily
immediately.
Wild garlic was in the air
when his owner stopped to stare
at his rump, and shout 'Salami!' –
whatever that meant. 'Salami!'

The White Bear and the Arctic Fox

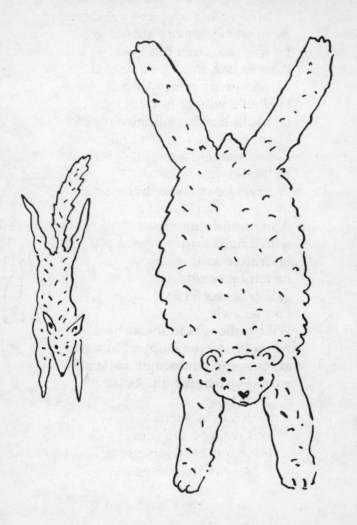

A white bear and an arctic fox
hid in a cave in the snow.
Men with guns were out there.
    They wished they'd go.

Bear looked at fox and said
'I wish we weren't white.
That's why they want us.
    We shine at night.'

Fox sneered and shook his tail.
'We're not in the sky.'
Then he stopped and said
    'Tell me why.'

Bear asked 'Are you crazy?
We can't get away.
This is our habitat.
    We can't fly.'

'We can't sit and wait here'
said the irate fox.
'Soon they'll be building
    apartment blocks

with ice, in Arctic City,
and we'll be the rugs.
If we don't do something
    we're dead mugs.

We can't go south, OK?
We need it white.
Where's whiter than the ball
    that shines at night?'

'But how do we get up there?'
asked the startled bear.
'And if we managed it
    would we have air?'

As they argued like this
the hunters found them
and before they could run
    they shot them.

Bees

Stung by a bee, he went running
and his cries brought more bees flying
in his zigzagging wake.
And for his peace-of-mind's sake
it was well he didn't know
they were hornets. There'd be no
escaping with swelling
accompanied by much yelling
if ten of their stings went in.
For him they were bees, and *one*
and *one only* had got him,
though most of the rest wanted him.

There were too many trees to dodge round,
and on such high ground!
Why had he gone for a wander
and decided to stop under
a tree where a bees' nest was hanging?
Why had he started poking
the nest with a stick?
At least he was quick
enough to realise, and to run
towards where the dawn sun
spotlit the roof of his car.
Key in hand, he lunged there.

Flies Carry Flu

Flies carry flu,
especially the small ones,
the hardly-seen-at-all ones
that sit on your hair
and wait there.

They wait till you
laugh or yawn
or make a vowel sound.
They aim above your chin
and rush right in.

They die, of course.
Spittle kills them
but the germ survives them,
the flu germ
that does you harm.

That keeps getting better
at making you iller,
that could be a killer.
So in case you die
get that fly.

A girl I know
thinks a spider
permanently inside her
mouth might do it.
She wouldn't need to glue it

to the roof, she says,
and she wouldn't mind the thought
of a web in her throat.
That's not much to do
to avoid flu.

I don't agree.
I'm sure you know
better ways to go
about it, easier ways
to clobber flies

and keep out flu.
So why don't you write
a letter tonight
telling me how.
You can start right now.

Cecil, the Spider

Cecil, the spider,
belongs to a boy
called Tom.
He lives at the top
of the coldwater tap
on the bath.
It's dry up there,
even when water
spurts out.
No room for a web –
Cecil doesn't care
a whit.
Tom feeds him
bits of hard skin
and toenails.
Cecil runs out
the tap's long spout
and drops
onto the bubbly
water's surface
and walks.
I bet you didn't know
spiders could walk
on water.
Or that they ate
bits of our skin
and toenails.

Or that a pipe
connects the taps
in England.
So if Cecil escapes
it might be you
he'll walk to
out of the steam,
eyeing the soles
of your feet.

The Doctor

Didn't the doctor drive the tractor well
        on his Dad's farm?
Didn't he love the pigs?
Where was a better place to sleep
than upstairs in the byre,
on a door nailed to the rafters,
warmed by the cows' breath?
But what about the doctoring?

No-one was sick, he said.
They were faking. That pain in the head
was a pain in the head, full stop.
Too much hair! Go to the barber shop!
That pain in the side? A stitch!
Even grannies ran too much.
Temperature? Stay away from the fire!
Even the man with one leg was a liar.

So he wouldn't drive his tractor
        to the hospital,
with half the townland in the trailer.
He wouldn't tell where he'd hid the syringe.
His stethoscope stayed on the neck of a horse
        and the people got worse
despite the doctor's Dad's attempts
at using the doctor's books
to diagnose and cure.
There was only one doctor
and he was some doctor,
a doctor on a tractor,
no doctor at all!

Mr Bluejack

Mr Bluejack likes the freezer,
sticks his head in when it's hot.
One son wants to do it also,
the other does not.

Mr Bluejack keeps a budgie,
calls it Greenface, sets it free.
One son wants it in the freezer,
the other won't agree.

Mr Bluejack's budgie, Greenface,
flies onto the frying pan.
One son can't imagine frying,
the other can.

Mr Bluejack lets his budgie
perch upon the chandelier.
One son loves its tuneless singing,
the other can't hear.

Mr Bluejack calls the freezer
Joe, and strokes its shiny door.
One son likes it less each day,
the other more.

Mr Bluejack wants his sons
to rear budgies of their own.
One son answers with a whoop,
the other with a moan.

Mr Bluejack stuffs the budgie
and both sons inside Joe.
One son pleads for Dad to join them,
the other whispers 'No!'

Parrot

Whose is that parrot on the streetlamp?
Why is he staring down like that?
Do we need such bright escapees?
Well, do we? Answer me that.

Answer me that – oh, there he goes
off to land on the next streetlamp,
the one that's on (it must be hot –
it is, he's off to another streetlamp,

I bet he'll sit there twice as long).
Look at His Brightness preening there
on a made-to-measure parrot perch.
I defy *you* not to stare.

You still haven't told me if you like it,
this burst into the pigeons' space
of green and red and curved beak
and eyes that stand out in his face.

There he goes, hopping streetlamps.
He means to do the whole street,
with a couple of minutes on each lamp
before he airlifts his feet.

Where is there an open window?
What'll he do at the street's end?
Haven't the cats sniffed his presence?
Doesn't he have a human friend?

Or did this friend open the cage
and say: 'Parrot, off you go,
the city's yours, come back if you want.'
Will he? He clearly doesn't know.

The Money Tree

Listen, there *is* a money tree.
I know you don't believe me,
and I didn't when Bill told me
that his mate Joe's brother
waters it every day.

It's not just water – there's sweat
and blood mixed in, not so's
you'd notice, Joe's brother says,
and he should know because
he mixes it himself.

There's another works with him,
another money-gardener
and they hate each other,
watch each other like dogs –
that's part of the job.

The tree is in a courtyard
surrounded by blank walls
with slits for rifles,
and a ceiling of perspex
that can slide open.

Where is this courtyard?
Joe's brother doesn't know.
Every morning he has to go
to a rooftop in the city
where a copter lands.

They put on a blindfold
and no-one speaks. They whirr
Joe's brother somewhere
in the city, he can't say.
It's best he can't.

Why is there only one tree?
That's what I want to know.
You'd think they'd grow
plantations of the stuff.
Joe's brother laughs.

He sees the look
on the faces that come
every weekday at noon
to collect the picked leaves.
They wouldn't share.

If you still don't believe me
come here and we'll go
see Bill, and then Joe
and then his brother,
and ask him yourself.

The Burglar

When the burglar went out
to burgle a house

When the burglar pulled on
his black polo-neck,
his beret, his Reeboks

When the burglar rattled
his skeleton keys,
checked he had his street-map,
said goodbye to his budgie

When the burglar shouldered
an empty bag, big enough
to take as much swag
as the burglar could carry

When the burglar waited
for the bus

When the burglar stood
at the bottom of the street
where the house he'd picked
to burgle was

When the burglar burgled
he didn't know
that another burglar
was inside *his* house

And only the budgie would see

Captain Hately

In that big house
  at the top of the drive,
    behind a locked door
Captain Hately prowls the top floor,
carrying a candle
  or a paraffin lamp
    from room to room,
leaning forward, peering through the gloom,
always listening
  for a key in the lock,
    the sound of a car,
always waiting, wondering where they are,
those four sons
  he raised alone,
    all gone away
and seldom, if ever, coming back to stay,
despite the gifts
  he's promised them
    with his own breath,
gifts they'll get in time, after his death –
for one, the island,
  one, the estate,
    another, his wealth,
for the fourth, his favourite, the house itself
with his grave ready
  by the chestnut tree
    on the front lawn.
And years of Captain Hately prowling on.

Gold

The gold bars lie buried in the silt
and three skeletons lie guarding them,
three males, though the squid who sleeps
in the first skull couldn't say
and couldn't care less. To her
it is a cave, a domed cavern
she shares with no-one. And who
could expect her to guess the plans
that had pulsed there, stalled,
till the ship reached Spain – expect her
to dream the face of the new wife
whose image had lodged there,
the image that faded with death?
The second skull lies yards away

from its long bones, and this one
is empty. But this one, too,
had taken in Spanish and spoken it out,
and had often eyed the gold.
Its eye-holes stare there still.
A crab sits in the third skull,
watching – a spider gone hard.
He is dictator of this stretch
of water, and the fact that he sits
in the skull of a Captain
is as useless to him as gold.
And nowhere on the skull wall
is a wisp of the knowledge
that the Captain's villa is ruined.
And the gold bars were going there
unknown to the crew. And unknown
to the divers whose boat churns above –
all they know is there's gold here.

Down the River

I got in my boat and went down the river,
    the full, flowing river,
    the river that goes through the jungle.

I paddled my boat down the river,
    the waving, winding river,
    the river that goes through the jungle.

I saw lots of wonders in that river,
    golden plants and golden flowers,
    a dead croc with a sword in it,
    a square box of diamonds,
    a starfish bigger than me,
    a diver looking for treasure,
    a machine-gun and a water-pistol,
    a big, golden teapot –

All these were in the river, and on the river
    was a ladder floating,
    a red, pink and orange rock,
    another, much bigger boat
    half-sticking out of the water,
    a swimming costume that fitted,
    a skipping rope I sprayed
    till it shone with gold,
    a sign saying 'Danger: Waterfall'.

I stuck to my boat in the river,
    the up and down river,
    the flooding, floating river.

I saw dangers around the river,
       a house that was alive
       and was trying to catch me,
       a dead bird falling down,
       black bumblebees flying
       and landing on a shot boy,
       a tail moving and a glimpse of eyes.

I kept on paddling down the river,
       the full, flowing river,
       the waving, winding river.

I saw an enormous diamond in the river,
       pink, green, orange and blue,
       colours changing in the sun.
       I stopped my boat by it,
       it was smooth and felt like china.
       I didn't want to climb on it,
       but some of the diamond fell off
       and I brought it home.

Home in my boat, down the river,
       the up and down river,
       the river that goes through the jungle.

Note: Written with the 1990 reception class of Aylward First and Middle School, after a performance by Peter Cutts.

The Ferryman

What's that over there? thinks the ferryman
as he makes for the shore.
Why are those people gathered?
Why are they shouting and cheering and laughing?
Why can't I be there?

And what's back behind us? thinks the ferryman
as he steers past a wreck.
Why are those car-horns hooting?
Why are the roads all jammed with queues?
Why can't I go back?

All these people standing at the rails
willing us ahead;
a crowd waiting and pushing,
calling me to hurry, some in the water!
I might as well be dead.

Over and back, back and over, always,
and staying nowhere!
Not even a stop for a meal,
or a swim, or a shave, or a chat on the phone,
neither here nor there.

Not even at night, thinks the ferryman
as he lassoes a rock
and holds the ferry fast,
and, with the noise from both shores growing,
makes his bed on the deck.

Mule

Somewhere in Indo-China
a sick man is strapped
to a three-legged mule.

His name is Aloysius,
his memory is used up
but the mule knows.

With each hop-step
down the dirt road
the man cries out.

The mule sees the city
through the miles of trees
and the many nights

for the mule never sleeps,
keeps hop-stepping on
with his feverish man.

When he gets tired
birdwinged butterflies
sip at his eyes.

When he feels lonely
troops of parrots
flash overhead.

All through the nights
the hospital lights
burn in the sky,

with the moon the theatre
where the surgeon waits.
The mule knows.